Mummy's HOME!

Christopher MacGregor and Emma Yarlett

PICTURE CORGI

Mummy's HOME!

For Vicky – a wonderful Mummy!
With love, C.M.

For you, Mum, with love always.
E.Y.

When my Mummy goes away,
We know she'll come home soon,
And when she's gone we'll miss her lots . . .
We LOVE her to the moon.

Before Mum leaves we'll help her pack —
We'll place her clothes in piles.

To make sure that she laughs each day
We'll bottle up our smiles.

I've made Mummy the softest toy

To keep her feeling bright

It's stuffed with cotton wool and love

It's a present for Mummy!

For cuddles every night!

We give each other special gifts
Of love to keep close by,

And when it's time for her to go
We'll stand and wave . . .

GOODBYE

In stormy seas or cast adrift
We'll play our pirate game –
As shipmates and *adventurers* . . .
We'll sail the climbing frame!

With Mummy gone we're incomplete,
There's puzzle pieces missing . . .

I wish she were at home with us
For cuddles, hugs and kissing!

To help us understand how long

Our Mummy's been away,

We'll fill a jar with *jellybeans*

And eat one every day!

To keep in touch we'll send our news
By letter and by phone.
It doesn't matter where she is,
My Mummy's linked with home.

TO: MUM@WORK.CC
FROM: FAMILY@HOM
SUBJECT: MISS YOU

What's cool about her trips away?
The surprises that appear,
Discovered while Mum's travelling
And -magicked- to us here!

My Mummy is
≡FANTABULOUS≡

She's BRILLIANT
through and through –

That's why she has to come and go

And help other people too.

My Mummy's gone away, you know,
But turning like the tide,
She'll rush back into our beach house
To be right by my side.

I know she *loves* me
more each day

The longer we're apart.

I feel it build
with every beat

Inside my little heart.

But if the colours drain away
To leave just black and white,

I'll talk it through with those I love

To make it feel all right.

When Mummy's back
we'll do FUN things

Like draw,

Ta Da!

and
make,

and sow.

We'll have a
picnic on the beach,
We'll help our garden grow.

My Mummy's coming home, you know,
And we'll decorate with flowers
To make our home look beautiful . . .

My Mummy's
coming home
today!

I can't believe
it's true.

A hug is worth

a thousand
words –

My kiss just . . .

I LOVE YOU!

Also available:

my DADDY'S GOING AWAY

* * *

For ideas, support and fun things to do, as well as to find out more about
Christopher MacGregor's inspiration and the true story behind this book,
please visit www.**mydaddysgoingaway**.com

MUMMY'S HOME! A PICTURE CORGI BOOK 978 0 552 56727 5
Published in Great Britain by Picture Corgi, an imprint of Random House Children's Publishers UK
A Penguin Random House Company

 Penguin
Random House
UK

This edition published 2015   10 9 8 7 6 5 4 3 2 1
Text copyright © Christopher MacGregor, 2015   Illustrations copyright © Emma Yarlett, 2015

RANDOM HOUSE CHILDREN'S PUBLISHERS UK 61–63 Uxbridge Road, London W5 5SA
www.**randomhousechildrens**.co.uk   www.**randomhouse**.co.uk
Addresses for companies within The Random House Group Limited can be found at: www.randomhouse.co.uk/offices.htm
THE RANDOM HOUSE GROUP Limited Reg. No. 954009
A CIP catalogue record for this book is available from the British Library.
Printed in China

MIX
Paper from
responsible sources
FSC® C020056

Penguin Random House is committed to a sustainable future for our business, our readers and our planet.
This book is made from Forest Stewardship Council® certified paper.